This Little Tiger book belongs to:

_____

_____

_____

For all my Little Hippos
— J S

For Grandma and Grandpa
— S P

LITTLE TIGER PRESS
1 The Coda Centre, 189 Munster Road, London SW6 6AW
www.littletiger.co.uk

First published in Great Britain 1999
This edition published 2014 by Little Tiger Press, London
Text copyright © Jonathan Shipton 1999
Illustrations copyright © Sally Percy 1999
Jonathan Shipton and Sally Percy have asserted their rights
to be identified as the author and illustrator of this work
under the Copyright, Designs and Patents Act, 1988

Printed in China • LTP/1900/0813/1013
2 4 6 8 10 9 7 5 3 1

How to be a Happy Hippo

Jonathan Shipton   Sally Percy

LITTLE TIGER PRESS

There was something wrong with Horace.
He had everything a small hippo could
possibly need.

Mountains of food . . .

lots of things to play with . . .

and plenty of mud!

But Horace wasn't a happy hippo.
There was something missing from his life.
But he wouldn't tell his sister what it was.
He wouldn't even tell his mother.
And as for his dad . . .

Well, you would have to catch Horace's dad first!
He always had someone to meet,
or somewhere else to go.
So Horace didn't get to see him much.

Sometimes Horace
heard his dad . . .
He even smelt him
once in a while . . .
And, if there was a blue moon, he sometimes got a kiss at bedtime.
But all this wasn't
enough for a
growing hippo.

Horace wanted to learn about crocodiles,

and how to walk along the bottom of
rivers without anyone noticing,

and how to hold his breath.

But, most of all, he just wanted a good,
long wallow with his big, round dad!

Poor Horace! He tried very hard to catch his dad . . .

but he had no luck at all!

Whatever Horace did, Mr. Hippo just wouldn't stop.
There was always someone to see or somewhere to go.
Horace got more and more upset.

Then one morning, when Horace
asked him to play, Mr. Hippo surprised
everyone by saying, "OK!"
"Yippee!" cried Horace, and he gave his
dad a big hug and asked him, "When?"
Mr. Hippo scratched his ear and said,

"Hmm, I think I can manage this afternoon."
Then he rushed off to work.

Horace was so excited he nearly burst!
He spent the morning getting everything ready.
He couldn't wait for his dad to come home.
What a happy hippo Horace was!

He waited and he waited.
He waited until the sun set.
He waited until the first star began to shine.
But still there was no sign of Mr. Hippo.

When Mrs. Hippo came to look for her little son,
she didn't have to ask him what was wrong.
Poor Horace was so upset there was only one
thing he could do.

He waited until all the big hippos
had gone to bed.
Then he tiptoed down the jungle
path in the pouring rain.

Halfway along the path Horace stopped.
He drew a circle in the mud and he began to dig.

And when the hole was very deep, he scrambled
out and carefully covered the top with sticks
and grass and leaves. Then he crept back
home again and fell fast asleep.

The next morning began with a loud
CRASH!
All the hippos rushed out, but Horace
was the quickest.

In fact, he was a bit too quick!
Before you could say,
"Help, Heavy Hippopotamus!"
Horace had fallen into his own hippo trap,
right on top of his . . .

. . . big, round dad!
Mr. Hippo looked at Horace,
and Horace looked at Mr. Hippo.
Mr. Hippo rubbed the dirt from
his eyes and snorted . . .

and then he burst out laughing.
He laughed and laughed
and laughed.

He picked up a great big lump of sticky mud and threw it at Horace.
So Horace picked up an even bigger, wetter lump and threw it back!

It must have been
wonderful mud, because
they carried on all morning.
You never saw such a pair
of happy hippos!

After lunch Horace and his dad
rolled on their backs and chatted
about big, round hippo things like
underwater bubbles and hairy legs,
and how to walk along river beds.

And then they did everything, all over again until . . .

. . . the moon rose and the first star came out.
By this time Horace was so tired that Mr. Hippo
had to carry him home to bed.

As Horace snuggled into bed, he opened
one sleepy eye and smiled at his big, round dad.
"I can't wait until tomorrow," he whispered.
"Neither can I!" whispered Mr. Hippo back.